A
Dolphin Named
Bob

A DOLPHIN NAMED

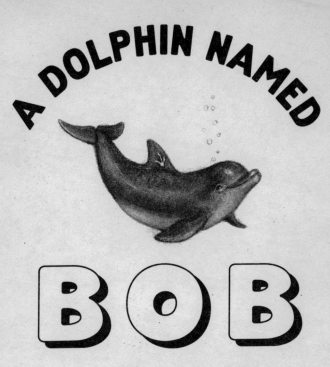

BOB

BY TWIG C. GEORGE

illustrated by Christine Herman Merrill

■ HarperCollins*Publishers*

For my mother, Jean Craighead George
—T.C.G.

Grateful acknowledgment is made to: Dr. Joseph R. Geraci,
Ontario Veterinary College, Guelph, Ontario, and Nedra Hecker,
Curator of Marine Mammals, National Aquarium in Baltimore

Library of Congress Cataloging-in-Publication Data
George, Twig C.
   A dolphin named Bob / by Twig C. George ; illustrated by Christine
Herman Merrill.
      p.   cm.
   Summary: A very sick dolphin is nursed back to health by the staff of a
marine aquarium and years later has a baby that becomes the star of the
show there.
   ISBN 0-06-025362-2. — ISBN 0-06-025363-0 (lib. bdg.)
   1. Dolphins—Juvenile Fiction.   [1. Dolphins—Fiction.]   I. Merrill,
Christine Herman, ill.   II. Title.
PZ10.3.G325Do   1996   95-8362
[Fic]—dc20   CIP
                                                                        AC

Typography by Steve Scott
1   2   3   4   5   6   7   8   9   10
❖
First Edition

Reprinted by arrangement with HarperCollins Publishers.

Table of Contents

1

A Strandling

Even before Bob was born, no one expected him to live, much less flourish. They might have guessed, though, that he would survive. His mother, Aster, was a dolphin with a remarkable will to live and a story of her own.

When Aster was about ten months old, she was washed ashore by a tremendous storm. For two days she lay stranded on the sand dune where the storm's powerful waves had left her. She could hear the sea, but she could only arch her body and inch her way toward the sound of the water. After many, many tries she grew too weak to move.

By the time a group of bird-watchers discovered her, she was almost dead. Her dove-gray skin was sunburned and coated with sand. Her breathing sounded like the wind blowing through the dry sea oats that surrounded her. It was the sound that attracted the attention of the leader of the bird-watching group, Mrs. Lee, who, luckily, was also a charter member of the Maryland State Aquarium's Marine Mammal Animal Rescue Program. Today, however, she was on the lookout for piping plover nests. She carefully climbed the dune, so as not to disturb the rare birds that she hoped to discover or the fragile dune grasses, and gasped.

"Over here," she called to her group. "Step carefully! Look, it's a very young dolphin, and it's still alive!" The kind woman shooed away the flies swarming around the dolphin's still form.

Digging a hole for its flippers, she rolled the dolphin on its side and examined its belly and tail flukes. "It's a female," she observed. "Lucy, Bill, get some towels from the car," she

2

ordered. "Soak them in the surf. The cool water will soothe her skin. It must hurt terribly." Aster's eyes roamed wildly over the group as they surrounded her. Then a cool, wet towel blocked them from sight.

The towels calmed Aster. She closed her eyes. Weak and dehydrated, she weighed less than the eighty to ninety pounds she had weighed at birth over six months ago.

Mrs. Lee, relying on her training from the Aquarium, quickly rolled the dolphin into the center of two large towels.

"Pick up the edges of the towels," directed Mrs. Lee. "We'll use them like a stretcher to carry her to the car. Leave a gap between the towels for her flippers. I'm going take her to the Aquarium. They may be able to help her."

Aster was too tired to struggle. Together, Lucy, Bill, and the other bird-watchers gently lifted the five-foot dolphin and carried her over the dunes to the parking area nearby. They placed Aster in the back of Mrs. Lee's huge, old station wagon and shut the rear door.

"Lucy," Mrs. Lee called as she slid into the driver's seat, "call the Aquarium and tell them I'm coming!"

"All right," Lucy shouted over the noise of the car's revving engine. "I'll call as soon as I find a phone!"

Then Mrs. Lee eased the car down the road and around the corner. Bird-watching was over for the day.

Three hours later Mrs. Lee arrived at the Maryland State Aquarium and was met by a group from the animal rescue program. Aster was taken from the car and placed in the capable hands of Mike, the head trainer and curator of the Aquarium's marine mammal program.

Mike was fit from his hours in the water with dolphins. He easily carried Aster to the quarantine pool: a quiet, dark pool completely separate from the rest of the pools in the Aquarium. It was used only for sick and injured marine animals. Aster's skin was full of sores, and the staff would soon find out that her body was plagued with a serious illness.

Motionless, she slid into the pool. The buoyant salt water held her limp body at an angle so that her blowhole rested above the surface. This allowed her to breathe with almost no effort. Aster's body was perfectly designed for the life of a marine mammal, an animal that breathes air but lives in the sea.

Though tall and strong, Mike was a gentle man with dark-brown eyes, a wide smile, and a patient, quiet way about him. Mike knew Aster was very ill and immediately called Dr. Lauren Manekin, the Aquarium veterinarian. Lauren, as she insisted on being called, was an energetic young woman with bright eyes and fine, curly hair that bounced when she moved or spoke. She had worked with many beached marine mammals, which are called "strandlings" because they are stranded on land, and was an expert on their particular health problems. Besides tending several Atlantic bottlenose dolphins, two Pacific bottlenose dolphins, and many seals, Lauren also cared for the Aquarium's collection of more than 5,000 fish, reptiles, amphibians, and birds. It was a demanding job and she loved it.

Mike watched Lauren examine the young calf and take blood samples.

"Will she make it?" he asked.

"I won't know until I get these blood samples to the laboratory," she answered. "You're right. She *is* a female. A young Atlantic bottlenose dolphin and she's not even a year old. Try and get her to take some freshwater. I'll be back as soon as I can."

Lauren hurried off to the lab. Mike got out a bottle with a long tube and filled it with water. Aster's eyes followed him as he moved around the cement deck that circled her pool.

He slid waist deep into the water and held Aster firmly, wrapping his arm behind her flipper. She was frightened. Her breathing was fast, and her eyes searched for a way out. There was none. If she had been stronger, even Mike would have needed the help of several other trainers to hold her. Instead, she let Mike slip the flexible tube into her mouth and, as he gently squeezed the water into her mouth, she had her first taste of freshwater. Dolphins do not drink seawater. It is too salty. Instead, they get all the fresh, unsalty water they need from the fish they eat or, at Aster's age, by nursing from their mothers. Since Aster had not been fed for many days, she needed water badly.

Two hours later Lauren was back with sheets of computer printouts from the lab. They made sense to her because of her years of experience in reading the blood tests of many marine animals.

"What did you find out?" Mike asked.

"It looks like a bacterial infection of the liver," Lauren explained. "The blood studies show that she's had the problem for some time."

"Can you help her?" Mike asked quietly, knowing full well that bringing a stranded dolphin back to health was very difficult and costly. Often an animal could not be returned to the sea because of health problems that could never be completely cured. For that reason, many strandlings became permanent residents of the Aquarium.

"Maybe I *can* help her," Lauren said. "Two years ago I would have said, 'I can't,' but I have a new antibiotic that works wonders. Want to try?" Nursing a dolphin or any stranded animal back to health was a team effort. She and Mike would have to work together.

Mike looked at the small, listless shape in the pool. Something about her told him she could make it.

"Okay," Mike said, "let's do it."

2

A Mind of Her Own

After many months of feeding and medical care and a lot of pampering from the trainers, Aster was doing better. However, as Mike had feared, she would never be completely healthy. Her liver was permanently damaged, and she would always need special care. She could never be sent home to her family group—her pod—now feeding somewhere off the East Coast in the Atlantic Ocean. She would never learn from her aunts and mother how to be part of the group or how to feed and live wild in the sea. Instead, she would learn from a smaller group of dolphins and their human trainers how to survive in two million gallons of water at the Aquarium's Marine Mammal Pavilion.

Lauren named the strandling Aster, after the hardy wildflower. Aster grew up under the huge glass dome that covered the Pavilion. The Pavilion was a handsome arena with five curved pools connected by underwater gates and surrounded by a stadium. One pool, the performance pool, was as big as a soccer field. It alone held over a million gallons of water. The smallest was the medical pool, where Aster was moved so she could be with the other dolphins while they continued to nurse her back to health. It was a long and tricky process because Aster was so young.

Once Aster regained her strength, it became clear that she had a mind of her own. On some days she was friendly and cooperative and responded to the eight other dolphins that lived in the Pavilion by tossing balls back and forth and exchanging a wide range of sounds. On other days she thrashed her tail from side

to side and clapped her jaws together, a motion called jaw popping, which warns away other dolphins. On these days she would not raise her flippers or flukes for her daily checkup, or jump in unison with the other dolphins during training sessions. She would jump alone, executing triple and quadruple flips across the enclosure. Then she would slap her flukes on the water's surface and create a commotion among the other dolphins in the Pavilion. The trainers knew Aster's moods and did not push her to cooperate. They just tried to calm the other dolphins and waited for Aster to join the group again.

But there were other days, sad days, when her diseased liver made her ill. On these days she refused to eat and her eyes became dull. Lauren, Mike, and the other trainers would bring her herring, capelin, and squid—all her favorite foods. They would talk to her and rub her down and worry. When she refused to eat, she did not get any freshwater, which further strained her liver. The staff would watch and wait, wishing she would return to her ornery, wonderful self.

Every day she was well, however, Aster would energetically perform the eleven- and four-o'clock shows.

As the people entered the stadium, they passed Aster's pool. When she saw them, she would slap her tail on the water, *crack!* Babies were startled and cried, and timid visitors scrambled for seats high up in the stands. The older children squealed and ran to the seats in the front rows marked SPLASH ZONE, hoping for more.

When the "leaping music" started, Aster entered the large pool with the other dolphins. She did a triple flip. Then another. The crowd was spellbound. As the music got faster, Aster leaped higher and higher. Finally she would soar out of the water 23 feet above the heads of the audience. The audience roared, and the children screamed with delight. And to top it all, when she landed, she sent a wave of water rolling over the side of the pool, dousing the kids and the few adventurous adults still sitting in the SPLASH ZONE.

Maybe she liked the feeling of being totally alone way up there in the sky. Maybe she liked the view. Maybe she caught a glimpse of the sea beyond the glass dome. No one really knew. What they did know was that Aster was always a great solo performer, a loner, and totally unpredictable. And that's the way it was for ten years, until something happened that changed all their lives. . . .

3

A Big Surprise

When Aster was eleven years old, she became pregnant.

Most dolphins get pregnant at eight years old, or maybe even at ten years old. Mike and Lauren had concluded that it would be better for Aster's health if she did not have a calf, and they thought they had done everything possible to make sure she did not get pregnant. But, as usual, Aster had her own plan—and this one almost killed her.

On the day of Aster's monthly blood test, the lab technician knocked on the door to Lauren's office.

"Come in, come in," she called as she hung up the phone. "What's up?"

"Aster is pregnant," blurted the technician, deciding it was best to get straight to the point.

"Pregnant?" Lauren repeated, astonished. "Test her again. This could be dangerous for her. Aster's not healthy enough to have a calf."

The second blood test was also positive. It was true. Aster was indeed pregnant. Lauren raced around the Aquarium and finally found Mike in the food-prep room. He was supervising the sorting of raw fish for the dolphins.

"Lauren." Mike smiled when he first saw her enter the room.

"Aster's pregnant," Lauren said abruptly. Mike stopped what he was doing; his eyes widened.

"How on earth . . ." Mike looked dumbfounded. "That's not good. She might not be able to carry a calf to full term in her condition. Twelve months is a long time."

"I know," Lauren confessed. "I'm worried

about her. With her liver problems she, or the calf, or both, might not survive the pregnancy. I'm also not sure how she will react to a calf. She might not take care of it." Lauren's brow wrinkled as she mentally began to run through the medical options for Aster.

Mike's thoughts ran in another direction. He knew that Aster's pregnancy would affect not only her but the other dolphins as well. He had to decide what was best for the whole group.

Dolphins have a complicated society. It consists of caring "aunties," who take care of their own calves as well as those of other females, or cows; dominant males, or bulls, who can be very rough; dominant females, who often have the most power of all, especially when they have calves; and the timid and weak that are constantly picked on.

As difficult as Aster was, she was Mike's favorite. He knew he could take Aster out of the shows and try to keep her quiet, but he also knew that would not be fair to Aster. Aster loved to perform, and taking that away from her would probably make her even more sickly. He could put her in the medical pool so that he could monitor her more carefully. But although Aster was a loner, she was very much a leader. The other cows depended on her aggressive manner to protect them from the larger, stronger males during the shows. When Aster was nearby, the males kept their distance. If Mike moved Aster, he might put some of the other females in danger. Every time a dolphin left the group or a new one joined it, there was turmoil while the group worked out a new social order. Aster, he decided, should stay with the group as long as she could during her twelve-month pregnancy.

For the next four months everything went well. Aster's appetite was good, and her jumps were as high as ever. Mike and Lauren watched her carefully. They could tell how she was feeling by the way her eyes looked, the way she ate, and how active she was.

Every day the staff worked with the dolphins, teaching them new tricks and having fun, too. They gave the dolphins balls to toss, and floats on ropes to tug and play with. To encourage good behavior and good relationships, they gave them special treats like rubbing their bellies and splashing their tongues with water. The dolphins and trainers were very attached to each other. Each dolphin had his or her own special skills and preferred particular rewards and trainers—all except Aster. It seemed she did what she did because she wanted to, not to please a trainer or earn a particular treat.

Aster loved to jump and touch a rubber ball that hung from the top of the stadium. She did this whether she got a reward or not. She jumped for reasons of her own, dolphin reasons, which people may never understand. To the trainers it looked as if she jumped for the sheer joy of it.

The dolphins were rotated in the five performances each day so they would not tire of the routine and stop performing. When Aster was feeling well, however, she performed during every show, whether she was in it or not. No matter which pool she was in, as soon as Aster heard the music begin, she would leap toward the sky beyond the dome. If she was in the performance pool, she would arc across the water, high above the heads of the audience. If she was in one of the other pens, she would jump as high as the size of the enclosure would allow.

When she wasn't leaping, Aster would tease the dolphins in the big pool who were waiting to perform their part in the show. Though they were separated by underwater gates, Aster learned to trill and click through the rubber-coated mesh. Instantly Tass and Beau, the two bull Atlantic bottlenose dolphins, who often performed together, would roll and surge around the tank. They clicked back and forth trying to find Aster with sound. Aster would click again. They often sent huge waves of water crashing over the sides of the pool, flooding the deck the trainers used for the demonstrations. The trainers often slid off the platform into the water.

The crowds would laugh and cheer, thinking the waves and the spills were part of the show. The trainers would roll their eyes, shrug their shoulders, and good-naturedly take it as part of the job. Aster would raise her head out of the water to click her approval.

4

A QUIET ARRIVAL

After four months Aster's health began to fail. As Lauren had feared, the growing calf was a strain on Aster's damaged liver. Aster stopped jumping and swam slowly around the pool. She rolled sideways and turned one eye up to the sky; then she rolled back.

Life in the Marine Mammal Pavilion became much quieter. The social order of the dolphin group changed. Because she was ill, Aster was no longer the protector of her group. Akai, a young cow, who had just given birth to a calf they named Kia, became the new leader. Mike and Lauren hoped Aster would learn from

Akai how to be a good mother dolphin. Instead, Aster became the outsider. She was chased and bumped by the other dolphins. Even Belle, another young pregnant cow who was usually timid, would sometimes nip at Aster's flukes.

Mike watched Aster carefully. Before he went home each day, he would look in her eyes, observe her movements, and check her skin for scratches. He would also look for less visible signs of stress that would tell him she was in danger.

At five months, the calf was large enough for Mike to feel it moving when he gave Aster her daily exam. Mike thought Aster could feel the calf too, because she stopped eating for almost a week and became very listless. Mike and Lauren knew they could lose her and the calf at this point. They traded shifts, watching her day and night. They fed her freshwater with the tube she was now used to using. After a nightmarish week, Aster began to eat again, and Mike and Lauren relaxed.

Akai, Belle, and the other dolphins continued

to harass Aster. They were not being cruel. They were acting out ageless patterns of behavior that have developed to keep their group healthy. In the wild, a sick or weak dolphin would have been driven out of the pod and would most likely die. At the Aquarium, Mike and Lauren had other options. They opened the underwater gate to the medical pool. Aster entered it without even a nod from Mike. She was too ill to defend herself. Alone in the little pool, she was safe.

During the rest of her twelve-month pregnancy, there were many days when Aster would not eat. The staff kept a close watch. Volunteers were scheduled to watch her at all times. It was a nerve-wracking time for Mike and Lauren.

Then one afternoon late in March, Aster began surfacing more often to breathe. As Lauren timed Aster's breathing, Mike noted her movements. The muscles across her belly tightened, then relaxed. She was ready to give birth.

At six o'clock Mike and Lauren took a

break for dinner, leaving Aster in the care of the other trainers. At seven they returned and took up their logs and stopwatches. Suddenly, Aster's muscles began pushing the calf down the birth canal. The contractions were intense; Mike and Lauren waited anxiously. There was not a sound in the stadium except the occasional blow from the other dolphins as they surfaced to breathe. At eight thirty P.M. on a cold, miserable, and windy night, Aster gave birth to her calf in the small, familiar pool, under the protective glass dome of the Marine Mammal Pavilion.

As the calf shot backward away from her body, Aster turned instinctively to help him to surface for his first breath. Dolphin calves are born tail first, unlike most mammals, so that they can surface to get their first breath of air through the blowhole on top of their heads as soon after they are born as possible. But Aster was not a skilled mother, and her clumsy efforts got in the way of the newborn's natural impulse to rise to the surface and breathe.

Aster tried to lift him with her cone-shaped snout, her rostrum. Though her rostrum was perfectly designed for slicing through the water at tremendous speeds, it was useless for lifting her calf to the surface. He slipped off the smooth, curved snout and became confused. He swam the wrong way—to the bottom of the pool instead of to the surface.

Aster tried again, but lifting the calf was like trying to lift a leaf from the bottom of a pond with a stick. Finally, while Aster rose to breathe, the little dolphin fluttered to the surface for his first breath. Then Aster did a strange thing. She pushed him down to the bottom of the pool. A bubble rose from his blowhole. Lauren and Mike froze. The calf turned and popped back up to the surface on his own. He was going to be all right.

Mike shook his head in answer to Lauren's unspoken question. Why had she pushed her calf down to the bottom of the tank? He had seen many dolphin mothers push their calves down to the bottom, even flip them out of the water, at this crucial moment. It might be a test to see if the calf had the strength to keep going, or to clear the birth fluids from the calf's blowhole and air passage. To Mike it was another dolphin mystery that no one fully understood.

By eight thirty-five P.M. the calf had survived to do what many just-born dolphin calves, at sea or in an aquarium, do not. He had gotten his first breath of air.

5

CALF IN DANGER

Aster's baby was the skinniest, strangest-looking Atlantic bottlenose dolphin calf the staff had ever seen. Most calves are round, and lightly marked from their fetal folds, which are caused by their curled position inside their mothers. These folds soon fill out and disappear. Their dorsal fins typically droop at birth but soon open like a butterfly's wings and stand up straight. Aster's calf looked crumpled, like a piece of wastepaper. His drooping dorsal fin did not straighten. He would have looked comical if his life had not been in such danger.

The only outward sign of this calf's future

was a white mark on his dorsal fin. It looked like a comet shooting through the sky. Mike noticed the mark and silently hoped that the comet would bring good luck. This calf needed it.

That Aster's calf was alive was a miracle, but to Mike and Lauren that just meant more worrying. The odd little dolphin was so thin that his rib cage was larger than his stomach. He needed his mother's rich milk but did not seem to know how to get it. This was the next crisis. Mike and Lauren waited. If he did not nurse, he would not live. It was that simple. Almost twenty-four hours went by and still the baby dolphin did not nurse.

Dolphins and whales don't have soft lips that make it possible for the babies to suck like other mammals. Instead, they have fringed tongues. The baby rolls its tongue into a tube and flattens it against the mother, forming a seal so the calf can nurse. A mother dolphin's milk-laden breast tissue lies between two layers of strong muscles. She tightens the muscles to squirt rich, fatty milk, almost like warm butter, into her calf's mouth. Every few minutes the calf passes by one of the two mammary folds on its mother's streamlined belly, to get a few more ounces of milk. For a baby dolphin, nursing is like swimming underwater and drinking out of a squeeze bottle at the same time. Calves nurse this way for two to three years before they learn to eat completely on their own.

By the following night even patient Mike became frustrated waiting for the tiny calf to nurse.

"It's right there," he shouted. "Go for it!"

There was no change for a moment; then, as naturally as if he had been doing it for hours, the calf rolled his tongue and nursed as Aster turned her belly toward him. Mike and Lauren looked at each other and laughed. Exhausted, they went to their homes to sleep.

The next day Aster and her calf were moved back to the communal pool with the other females and calves. Aster quickly became the leader again with a few nips to show her strength and with her calf at her side.

There were now three new calves in the pool. Chessie, Belle's calf, had been born while Aster was in the medical pool. The Aquarium's pod was growing quickly.

Mike and Lauren knew that the calf's health would probably be poor for the next two years and possibly, like Aster's, his entire life. They watched the pair closely for the next few days for any signs that something was wrong. It was soon clear that there *was* a problem. Even though the little calf nursed often, he was getting thinner and thinner. He seemed to shrink before their eyes. The shape of his skull and each rib became visible, while Kia and Chessie grew fatter and rounder by the day.

Mike and Lauren feared that Aster was not able to provide enough milk for her calf. He was nursing but not gaining weight. Again the calf's life was in danger. He had to gain weight soon or he would die. In desperation Mike crawled into the small viewing room below the surface of the pool. It was used for observing the dolphins underwater at close range. He watched for a long time. Finally he had to accept that Aster could not feed her calf. The calf passed Aster. He nursed for a longer time than Mike had ever seen before. He knew it was because only a drop of milk was squeezed into the calf's mouth.

Aster was not making enough milk to feed her baby. The baby was slowly starving, and there was nothing anyone could do. Aster would not let them near her new calf. The other mothers would let their favorite trainers play with their calves and even, in some cases, feed them with a bottle if necessary, but not Aster. She charged Mike and all the other trainers when they came anywhere near her baby.

Lauren sadly watched Aster and her calf circle the pool together.

"Maybe this is why she stranded when she was young," Lauren said to Mike, who was standing with her. "It might be a genetic problem."

"It's possible," said Mike. "There's no way to know." The two experts watched the two dolphins helplessly.

Finally Mike decided he had to try to feed the baby in spite of Aster. For two days he sat with his feet in the water to try to relax Aster. The third day he slipped into the pool and stood motionless. The other females swam over with their calves for their treats and rubs, but Aster only eyed Mike suspiciously as she circled the pool with her calf.

Slowly Mike moved toward Aster. Lauren held her breath and looked on. Suddenly Aster sliced by Mike at top speed. The force of the water knocked Mike against the wall. He did not climb out. Aster darted at him again, this time with an open mouth revealing two rows of cone-shaped teeth, teeth she often used to rake the backs and flukes of dolphins that displeased her. Now they were threatening Mike.

"Mike," Lauren called firmly, "get out!"

Mike left the pool. He did not want to test Aster further. If she hurt him, their relationship might never be the same. He would never be able to trust her completely, and she would sense that.

Each day Mike, Lauren, and the entire Aquarium staff came to work hoping that Aster's odd little calf was still alive. They called him Bob because they were so happy to see him bobbing up and down next to his mother each morning.

As skinny and undernourished as he was, Bob was determined to live. He would swim right next to his mother hour after hour, and never seemed to tire. In the wild, newborn calves that cannot keep up with their pod are left behind. Bob would not have been one of these. Like a beacon of hope, the comet on his fin gleamed each time he surfaced for a breath. The staff watched and waited, hoping that Aster's milk would come in and allow Bob to live. They liked him.

Just when it seemed there was no hope for Bob, one of the other cows, Anani, surprised everyone. She was an experienced mother who had given birth to many calves. Her most recent calf had stopped nursing months ago. But something very special happened. One day as Bob swam by her, she responded by squeezing a stream of milk into his mouth.

After that, every five or ten minutes Bob swam by for a squirt of Anani's milk.

As soon as Anani began to nurse Bob, Aster began to make more milk. This seemed in keeping with her ornery personality, though the real reason would remain another dolphin mystery. Now Bob had two mothers to feed him, and that suited him just fine. He finally began to gain weight and grow.

Mike and Lauren were elated. Not only was Bob out of danger for now, but they were able to see and film Anani nursing a calf that was not her own. Though a few scientists had written about this rare behavior, no one at the Aquarium had seen it before. Now Mike and Lauren had a film that would help others understand more about dolphin behavior.

In just a few months Bob looked as healthy as the other calves. He would swim next to Anani for a while and then next to Aster. His comet mark grew as his dorsal fin straightened up. He was playful and full of energy, and very much alive.

6

BOB

It soon became obvious to Lauren and Mike and the other trainers that Bob was an original. Maybe it was because he had to look out for himself from the beginning, or maybe it was because he had an ornery mother. Bob was different from the other dolphin calves. At just three months he was a little more than a yard long, which is normal for a dolphin calf; but he was also most certainly his own boss, which is unusual.

He showed his independence in everything he did. Kia and Chessie, the two other calves, always swam right next to their mothers. If they strayed more than a flipper's length away, their mothers would blow, click, or chirp, and the calves would immediately return. Side by side they would rise, breathe, and dive in perfect unison. Cow and calf looked like reflections of each other.

But not Bob. No matter how much Aster and Anani blew, clicked, and huffed, Bob paid them no attention. When they called, he'd go off and explore the gate to another pool or the pipe hole where the water came into the tank. He would also follow the trainers as they walked around the rim of the pool, buckets of fish clanging together as they carried them to feed the dolphins. Sometimes he harassed Akai and Belle by leaping out of the water and flopping on their blowholes as they surfaced. He chased Kia and Chessie away from their mothers, blew bubbles under their bellies, and generally created chaos in the small community of dolphins. Only when he was quite ready would he swim back to his mothers.

In many ways Bob was like Aster, but in one

very important way he was not. He was truly interested in people. Whenever he saw one of the trainers by the edge of the pool, he would swim over for a back scratch. He watched Mike and learned quickly how to toss balls to him and make him laugh. Sometimes the staff wondered who was training whom.

One day Bob imitated one of his mother's leaps and Mike instantly blew on the high-pitched training whistle he and the staff always wore around their necks. The whistle meant "good job" to the dolphins. He reinforced the jump with a playful splash into Bob's mouth. Bob liked the mouth splash and clicked and squealed for more. Mike walked away to let Bob know that he was done.

Bob turned and swam back to his mother. Aster leaped again, so Bob did too. Mike was watching closely over his shoulder. As soon as Bob leaped, he turned and blew the whistle again. Bob recognized the signal and sped over so Mike could splash his mouth. His training had begun.

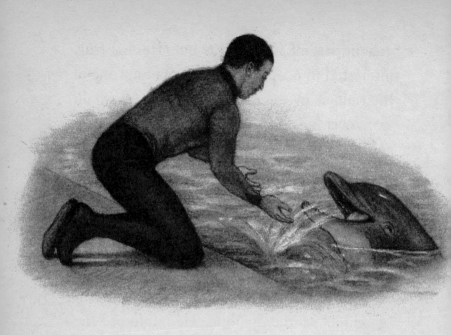

To encourage dolphins to repeat certain behaviors, trainers blow their whistles and give "reinforcers," things the dolphins like, such as back scratches and herring. There are also many behaviors that the trainers do *not* want to see repeated. Bob was equally good at doing both.

One day Bob began to leap on top of Akai, Belle, and Anani each time the trainers signaled them to leap. Every time he interrupted the session, the trio surged around the tank making huge waves. Bob loved the commotion he created.

Mike arrived and took in what was happening. He frowned at Bob, then nodded to the other trainers to start again. Just as Anani was about to leap out of the water, Bob swam right in front of her. Anani swerved and just missed Bob, and then, agitated, she vaulted around the pool. Bob saw Mike and sped over for his usual rub and splash. But Mike folded his arms, stood perfectly still, and looked over Bob's head. Bob did not like being ignored. He clicked and whistled, but Mike would not look at him. It was a dolphin "time out."

"Try it again," Mike called to the other trainers after several minutes. This time when Anani jumped, Bob did not get in the way. Mike splashed and rubbed him. He was a fast learner. The next day Bob jumped for Mike on command and streaked over for his mouth splash. At that moment, a tour group interrupted Mike. When Mike turned back to Bob, the little dolphin would not look at him. Mike had not done what Bob expected. Bob gave Mike a "time out."

"Well, well," Mike said, and laughed. "I guess it works both ways, doesn't it, Bob?"

Bob learned many things. Dolphins can locate objects underwater with sound as well as sight. He would make a clicking sound with his blowhole and then listen to the infinitesimal differences in the echoes to find tiny bits of fish and his favorite dolphin toys that had fallen to the bottom of the pool. This is called "echo-location." Sailors use sonar in much the same way to "see" reefs, sand bars, and even fish under the water. Bob quickly became a master at finding small objects by echolocation. One afternoon he found a small piece of paper that a visitor had thoughtlessly dropped. He pushed it over to Lauren on his rostrum.

"Why thank you, Bob," she said, scratching Bob's head as she took the small present.

Bob disappeared and brought back a dime. This time a visitor's prank could have endangered the dolphins. Coins are made of zinc, copper, and nickel and are very dangerous for marine mammals. They can get caught in animals' throats or lodge in their stomachs, where they dissolve and make them sick or even kill them. Lauren worried that, though Bob's tricks could be very helpful, he might be harmed by the coins. With careful training Bob learned to "point" out the coins and help collect the toys and occasional feeding bucket that fell in the pool.

Soon, Bob was a regular "cleaning genie." He would round up hula hoops, balls, and rope toys for the trainers. He had made up a game for himself that also kept the pool clean and safe for the other dolphins. Bob's antics were not all bad for the community of dolphins.

7

A FLYING LEAP

Every day the dolphins and the Aquarium staff put on five shows called behavior programs. Starbuck and Kona, the big male Pacific bottlenose dolphins, who were normally kept by themselves, and their smaller, lighter-colored cousins, the Atlantic bottlenose dolphins, would show the public what dolphins do at sea. In the Aquarium, as in the wild, dolphins leap, dive, spin, and communicate with an array of sounds and gestures.

During the show the bulls would "porpoise"—swim at high speed, just breaking the surface to breathe. With soft cups covering

their eyes, they would find small rings in the water using echolocation. They would even play with their trainers, pushing them around the pool and sometimes rocketing them fifteen feet into the air on the tips of their rostrums.

Aster had not performed since she had become ill when she was pregnant with Bob. And Lauren was still watching Aster's and Bob's health closely. However, now that Aster was feeling better, she was back to her old tricks and found many ways to create her own shows without officially being part of a performance. Just like old times, when Aster heard the trainers getting the buckets of fish ready for the program, she would go to the gate of the big pool, slap her tail, make clicking noises, and jaw-pop. The dolphins in the other pools would hear her and grow terribly excited.

Dolphin groups, even at the Aquarium, are made up of animals that have learned to live together. Some are leaders, like Aster and Akai, and some are followers, like Belle and Anani. There are the smart and the not-so-smart, the aggressive and the meek. Beau and Tass, the older Atlantic bottlenose bulls, tended to stay together, as did Starbuck and Kona. The females and young dolphins like Aster, Belle, Anani, and Akai also formed a social group. There were twelve dolphins divided into three groups at the Aquarium. Each group had worked out a communal peace—that is, until Aster would click and jaw-pop and provoke the other dolphins. Then Beau and Tass would slap their flukes and churn through the water, while the others responded with their own tail lobs and flipper flaps. Within moments all the dolphins would be porpoising around their pools. Aster caused pandemonium in the Pavilion.

Whenever Aster stirred up the dolphins, the trainers would have to calm them down again before they could start the show. Although they were happy that Aster was feeling like her old self, she was driving them crazy. Still, until Lauren was absolutely sure that both Bob and Aster were as healthy as possible, she did not want Aster to perform.

One day Aster heard the music for the high jumps. In her pool she vaulted up, down, and back up again. The audience cheered and clapped.

Then Bob started jumping with the music, too. At first he made his usual small, awkward leaps, landing on his mother and Anani. Then Kia and Chessie imitated Bob and started leaping around the pool with him. Soon, however, they became interested in blowing bubbles with their mothers instead and stopped. Not Bob. He jumped through every show. He jumped in the morning, and during the training sessions. Soon the spunky little dolphin was leaping higher than the other, bigger calves.

One day he sailed higher than he ever had before. While he was high above the heads of the trainers, he must have taken a good look at the other pools. Moments later, without any warning, he leaped out of the nursery tank, over the trainers, across a platform, and into the big performance tank!

The crowd went wild. They thought it was

part of the show. Mike was shocked. Nothing like this had ever happened before. The young calf had just leaped into a tank with Starbuck and Kona, the two 700-pound male Pacific bottlenose dolphins. If attacked or angered, bull dolphins are known to ram and even kill other dolphins by driving their rostrums into them at 25 miles an hour.

Mike was terrified for Bob. He immediately blew his whistle and signaled Starbuck and Kona to leave the performance tank.

They were hardly gone when Aster, realizing what had happened, came barreling over the wall after Bob. There they were, mother and calf in a million gallons of water. Bob had never seen so much water. He must have been a little startled, because for once he stayed close to Aster's side. He didn't jump or roll. He just swam flipper to flipper with her.

This charming display for the visitors soon became a disaster for the Aquarium.

8

A MILLION
GALLONS OF WATER

Two days later, Aster and Bob were still
swimming happily in the big pool. Try as they
would, the trainers simply could not get Bob
back to the nursery tank. He had not learned
to swim through gates, so they could not signal
him to return. He was too young to eat fish, so
they could not lure him through the gate with
a nice fat herring, and since Aster had milk
again, he did not need gentle Anani. He was
perfectly happy right where he was.

Mike and Lauren tried everything they could

think of to get him out of the big pool. They stood still and gave him the cold shoulder, but Bob didn't seem to notice. He had discovered a trick of his own. He would slap his tail at the edge of the tank, which sent a shower of water down on the visitors. The visitors scrambled and hooted, and went home to tell their friends they had been splashed by a baby dolphin.

When the cold shoulder did not work, Lauren and Mike tried to lure him back with mouth splashes. But that was dull compared to the new games he could play. The big pool had an underwater viewing window in the lobby, where people watched the dolphins swim. When children ran past the window, Bob would follow them at eye level from one end of the 70-foot window to the other. This was more fun than mouth splashes.

Aster, always protective, would nod a warning to the children to stay away from Bob. But since all dolphins have a jawline fixed in what looks like a permanent smile, her warning nod looked like "Yes, go ahead and play" to the

spellbound children. Back and forth they ran
with Bob until their parents grew tired of the
game and dragged them away.

Aster quickly found she could still control
the other dolphins from the big pool, by jaw
popping and clicking at the gates. Just as
before, they rolled, spun, and swam faster and
faster. Several times water sloshed up on the
platform, almost washing Lauren into the
pool. Mike just laughed and shook his head.

"Don't you wish you knew what Aster was saying to the other dolphins?" he asked Lauren.

"I think I know," Lauren said. "She's saying, 'Na-na a boo boo.' I believe that is universal language for 'You can't catch me.'"

As if in response, Aster slapped her flukes on the surface, making a cracking sound. The noise was earsplitting. (Noise travels better through water than through air.) The other dolphins swirled and slapped their tails. Chaos and Aster reigned at the Aquarium, and Mike and Lauren decided to cancel the shows until Bob could be removed from the tank.

9

DIVERS TO THE RESCUE

A week later the director of the Aquarium called Mike into his office.

"Mike," the director began, "people are complaining because there are no dolphin shows."

"I know, sir," Mike answered. "I am trying everything I can think of. This is an unusual situation, and a tough one to fix."

"I have an idea," offered the director. "Let's call in all our volunteer divers. They can surround Aster and her calf and guide them back into the nursery pool."

"That might work," replied Mike cautiously, "but you have to understand Aster and Bob.

They are not the most cooperative dolphins."

"Do you have a better idea?" asked the director.

"No, sir," Mike admitted.

"Well then, I want you to give it a try."

"Okay," said Mike reluctantly. Since he wasn't sure what else could be done, he felt he had to go ahead with the director's plan.

Early the next morning, forty volunteers in flippers and wet suits rimmed the edge of the performance pool. Mike explained what they were to do. They would get into the water and make a human net across the pool by linking arms. Then they would slowly try to ease Bob toward the gate. Knowing Aster and Bob, Mike did not have much confidence in the plan, but at this point he was willing to try almost anything.

Mike signaled the divers to slide into the water and link arms. Slowly they began to close in on Bob. Aster saw what was happening. She clicked and nodded a warning. Mike watched her closely. So far, she was just giving them a mild warning; but if Aster thought Bob was in danger, there could be big trouble. The divers started closing in. Aster warned them again, but they kept coming.

Suddenly Aster pumped her flukes and streaked by the line of divers. They saw only a streak of gray out of the corners of their eyes and then felt the impact of her wake in the water. From where Mike was standing he could see she had passed only inches from some of the divers. He blew his whistle and ordered the divers out. Forty divers encased in black rubber wet suits hauled themselves out of the water and up onto the training platform. They looked just like a herd of frightened sea lions.

As soon as the divers had gotten out of the water, Aster circled the pool with Bob. She rolled onto her side and looked Mike right in the eye as she passed him. Then slowly she rolled back, whacked the surface once with her flukes, soaking Mike, and dove to the bottom of the pool. Bob followed and found a new group of children to play with behind the underwater viewing window.

Mike knew Aster would not allow the divers to try again. With a sigh he sent them all home and went to report the results to the director.

10

THE SHOW
MUST GO ON

A month later Bob was six months old and
the staff gave up all plans for a simple solution.

"Aster," Mike announced one morning,
"will do the show. Her health is so good right
now, she is performing anyway, and as they say,
'the show must go on.'"

The next day visitors filled the stadium
again. The music started, and Aster followed
Mike's signals. She porpoised, caught and
found rings, and did quadruple flips and triple

rolls. She did five shows a day. The people cheered, but they could see the other dolphins in the back pools, and they complained: They wanted to see more dolphins, or they wanted their money back.

Attendance began to drop again. The staff was discouraged. Meanwhile, so slowly at first that no one really noticed it, Bob grew bolder. When the shows started, Bob would flip and jump as he had in the nursery tank. People clapped for him, and he became more adventurous. He jumped onto his mother's blowhole, his favorite game, and twirled in the water with her. He spy-hopped, raising his head above the water to see what was going on above the surface. He nodded his head up and down and clicked and whistled. The audience loved him. He flapped his flippers and flukes, saying, "I'm here," in dolphin talk. But Bob was a long way from being trained. He put on a show only when he felt like it.

One night Mike stopped by the Aquarium

on his way home from dinner. He liked to visit the Pavilion in the evening and often dropped in to enjoy the solitude. The humidity from the 70° water filled the stadium, and there was a sweet, salty smell to the air. He sat down to enjoy the peacefulness of the Aquarium at night. He was worried about Aster and Bob. He needed time to think. There had to be some solution he had overlooked.

The lights were off so that the dolphins could rest. He could hear the sound of their blows as they napped on the surface. Then he also heard a rhythmic *splash, splash, splash.* Concerned, he walked down to the big pool to investigate.

As his eyes adjusted to the light, he gasped. Bob was tossing a big ball to Kia in the nursery pool; she caught it on her rostrum and tossed it back. They were playing catch. Mike smiled and shook his head. He had tried for weeks to teach Kia to play ball. It looked as if Bob had succeeded where he had not.

The next day Mike hurried to the Aquarium

and threw the ball to Bob. He motioned for him to throw it over the gate to Kia. Bob did. Kia tossed it back.

"Now," Mike said, "if you could only teach yourself to jump back into that pool, you would spare me a lot of trouble!"

Mike started Bob's formal training. Bob was very young, but he was also a very quick learner. Like other smart dolphins he learned quickly, but he would test the trainers and change the behaviors as he learned new things. Kia and Chessie would be harder to train, but

Mike knew that once they learned something, they would do it exactly the same way each time. With a dolphin like Bob you never really knew what would happen. But maybe, just maybe, he could teach Bob to get himself out of that pool.

Now every time Bob jumped, Mike gave him the hand signal he had been using casually. Soon Bob was jumping regularly at Mike's commands. But he would not jump back into the nursery tank.

The training continued. Mike held out a long pole with a round rubber float at the end called a target. He slapped the target on the water, then held it just above the surface. Bob leaped up through the spot where the target had hit the surface, then touched the target with his rostrum. Each day Mike taught Bob to follow the target higher and higher.

Now Bob watched for Mike to arrive each day. He clicked and swam to him as soon as he reached the edge of the pool. Bob would bring Mike presents of the toys he found. Mike thanked Bob with soft talk, rubs, and mouth splashes. Soon when Mike slapped the surface with the target, Bob knew to soar out of the water and arc high over Mike's head to touch the rubber float before entering the water again with barely a splash. He *was* a smart dolphin. In spite of everything, Mike was proud of him.

Alas, smart as Bob was, Mike could not teach him to go over the wall or in and out of the gates between the pools. Bob did not want to swim through the narrow passage. In the wild, dolphins instinctively avoid tight spaces, so going through the gate was a behavior that took a long time to teach.

Every time the trainers tried to get Bob to go through the gate, he would arch his back and stop short. It was almost as if there were an invisible shield across the gate. Aster was signaled to swim through the gate to show Bob it was okay. Mike and Lauren even jumped in and swam back and forth themselves—nothing worked. Each time Bob got to the gate, he stopped. He simply would not go through.

For two months most of the seats in the Pavilion were empty. People who had traveled long distances to see all the dolphins perform were annoyed. Children were disappointed. The staff was worried.

11

A Star Is Born

Several days later the director called a meeting of the entire staff. When everyone had arrived and settled into the seats, he opened the meeting.

"The mayor called me yesterday," he began, speaking very slowly so that each of the staff members understood that this was not an ordinary meeting. "He is going to bring some very important guests to see the dolphins perform in *two weeks*. All the dolphins must perform. We must get Bob out of that pool!"

Mike's stomach tightened. He looked over at Lauren. She looked at him. They both looked worried. There was complete silence. Finally Mike spoke up.

"We'll do what we can, sir." But he doubted that they could do much more than they were already doing. It took months to train older dolphins to do things that were much more natural than what they were asking young Bob to do. The meeting ended. Everyone knew what was expected. They must get Bob and Aster out of the performance pool.

The trainers went to work. All day long they coaxed, trained, splashed, and rubbed Bob, but nothing would get him through that gate. Finally Mike dove in and grabbed him, but the powerful flukes and silicon-smooth skin made him impossible to hold. Bob wriggled free. They even tried coaxing him onto the platform, over the wall . . . anything. Nothing worked.

The day of the mayor's visit arrived. The mayor and his guests seated themselves in the front bleachers. As Aster began the show, the mayor looked concerned.

As the show went on, the mayor scowled. The staff was nervous. The director looked furious. And then, as Aster began doing her twirls, Bob joined her. He twirled and jumped, flapped his pectoral fins against his side, and flopped on his mother. The crowd cheered. The mayor smiled briefly. The director looked hopeful.

Mike worked frantically and Bob performed beautifully. He and Bob went through every behavior they had ever worked on.

Finally, when the music rang out for the high leaps, Mike crossed his fingers and signaled Bob to leap. Bob did not react. He seemed to have forgotten the behavior they had worked the hardest on. Mike was frantic. Thirteen hundred people and the mayor were waiting expectantly.

Mike crossed his fingers, folded his arms, and looked up at the dome, ignoring Bob. The music pounded on as the audience waited. Mike took a deep breath and tried again. He signaled, Bob hesitated . . . and then took off.

With each jump, he leaped higher and higher. When the time came for the final leap, he soared higher than his mother, higher than he ever had. The mayor, the director, and the visitors stood and roared their approval. Mike and Lauren beamed. The other trainers cheered.

And then Bob was done. With a flash of his tail he soared over the platform and back into the nursery pool. Aster circled the gigantic enclosure once as if to say good-bye and jumped over the wall too. It was a spectacular finale. The mayor clapped enthusiastically.

"Well, well," Mike said, "he did teach himself to get back into that pool after all. I guess I should have expected that."

That day Bob, the little dolphin no one had even expected to live out his first day, had become the star of the Aquarium.

AUTHOR'S NOTE

The story of Bob and Aster is based on the real lives of several dolphins. Just like Bob and Aster, every dolphin is unique. Each has his or her own personality, physical characteristics, and role to play in the social group. At the same time, like all species, dolphins share many things in common, whether they live in a marine park or aquarium or at sea.

It is my hope that the next time you are lucky enough to see dolphins, you will watch them with a new appreciation and curiosity— and that you will always want to know more about what they really mean with their tail lobs, their whistles, and their wonderful smiles.